A System of National Education

MAXWELL PRESS

A SYSTEM OF NATIONAL EDUCATION

Aurobindo Ghose

MAXWELL PRESS

Chennai   New Delhi

MAXWELL PRESS

An Imprint of MJP Publishers

ISBN 978-93-5528-063-3 **MAXWELL PRESS**

All rights reserved
Printed and bound in India
No. 44, Nallathambi Street,
Triplicane,
Chennai 600 005

MJP 1411   © Publishers, 2022

Publisher :   **C. Janarthanan**

PUBLISHER'S NOTE

The legacy of a country is in its varied cultural heritage, historical literature, developments in the field of economy and science. The top nations in the world are competing in the field of science, economy and literature. This vast legacy has to be conserved and documented so that it can be bestowed to the future generation. The knowledge of this legacy is slowly getting perished in the present generation due to lack of documentation.

Keeping this in mind, the concern with retrospective acquiring of rare books has been accented recently by the burgeoning reprint industry. MAXWELL PRESS is gratified to retrieve the rare collections with a view to bring back those books that were landmarks in their time.

In this effort, a series of rare books would be republished under the banner, "MAXWELL PRESS". The books in the reprint series have been carefully selected for their contemporary usefulness as well as their historical importance within the intellectual. We reconstruct the book with slight enhancements made for better presentation, without affecting the contents of the original edition.

Most of the works selected for republishing covers a huge range of subjects, from history to anthropology. We believe this reprint edition will be a service to the numerous researchers and practitioners active in this fascinating field. We allow readers to experience the wonder of peering into a scholarly work of the highest order and seminal significance.

MAXWELL PRESS

CONTENTS.

PUBLISHERS NOTE.

The Publishers have much pleasure in presenting this volume which is but a compilation of a series of articles from the pen of Srijut Aurobindo Ghose contributed several years ago. In view of the fact that much interest and enthusiasm are evinced at the present moment in National Education the Publishers trust that the main theme enunciated by India's greatest yogi in this book will be of immense use in guiding the army of nation-builders in their re-modelling of the Education of the youth of the country.

A System of National Education

I. THE HUMAN MIND

The true basis of Education is the study of the human mind, infant, adolescent, and adult. Any system of Education founded on theories of academic perfection, which ignores the instrument of study, is more likely to hamper and impair intellectual growth than to produce a perfect and perfectly equipped mind. For the Educationist has to do, not with dead material like the artist or sculptor, but with an infinitely subtle and sensitive organism. He cannot shape an educational masterpiece out of human wood or stone ; he has to work in the elusive substance of mind and respect the limits imposed by the fragile human body.

There can be no doubt that the Educational System of Europe is a great advance on the many methods of antiquity, but its defects are also palpable. It is based on an insufficient knowledge of human psychology and it is only safeguarded in Europe from disastrous results by the refusal of the ordinary student to subject himself to the processes it involves, his habit of studying only so much as he must to avoid punishment or to pass an immediate test, his resort to active habits and vigorous physical exercise. In India the disastrous effects of the system on body, mind and character are only too apparent. The first problem in a National System of Education is to give an Education as comprehensive as the European and more thorough, without the evils of strain and cramming.

This can only be done by studying the instruments of knowledge and finding a system of teaching which shall be natural, easy and effective. It is only by strengthening and sharpening these instruments to their utmost capacity that they can be made effective for the increased work which modern conditions require. The muscles of the mind must be thoroughly trained by simple and easy means; then, and not till then, great feats of intellectual strength can be required of them.

The first principle of true teaching is that nothing can be taught. The teacher is not an Instructor or Taskmaster, he is a helper and a guide. His business is to suggest and not to impose. He does not actually train the pupil's mind, he only shows him how to perfect his instruments of knowledge and helps and encourages him in the process. He does not impart knowledge to him, he shows him how to acquire knowledge for himself. He does not call forth the knowledge that is within; he only shows him where it lies and how it can be habituated to rise to the surface. The distinction that reserves this principle for the teaching of adolescent and adult minds and denies its application to the child is a conservative and unintelligent doctrine. Child or man, boy or girl, there is only one sound principle of good teaching. Difference of age only serves to diminish or increase the amount of help and guidance necessary, it does not change its nature.

The second principle is that the mind has to be consulted in its own growth. The idea of hammering the child into the shape desired by the parent or teacher is a barbarous and ignorant superstition. It is he himself who must be induced to expand in accordance with his own nature. There can be no greater error than for the parent to arrange beforehand that his son shall develop particular qualities, capacities, ideas, virtues, or be prepared for a pre-arranged career. To force the nature, to abandon its own *dharma* is to do it permanent harm, mutilate its growth and deface its perfection. It is a selfish tyranny over a human soul and a wound to the Nation, which loses the benefit of the best that a man could have given it and is forced to accept instead something imperfect and artificial, second rate, perfunctory andcommon. Every one has in him something divine, something his own, a chance of perfection and strength in however small a sphere which God offers him to take or refuse. The task is to find it, develop it and use it. The chief aim of Education should be to help the growing soul to draw out that in itself which is best and make it perfect for a noble use.

The third principle of Education is to work from the near to the far, from that which is to that which shall be. The basis of a man's nature is almost, always, in addition to his soul's past, his heredity, his surroundings, his nationality, his country, the soil from which he draws sustenance, the air which he breathes, the sights, sounds, habits to which he is accustomed. They mould him not the less powerfully because insensibly, from that then we must begin. We must not take up the nature by the roots from the Earth in which it must grow or surround the mind with images and ideas of a life which is alien to that in which it must physically move. If anything has to be brought in from outside, it must be offered, not forced on the mind. A free and natural growth is the condition of genuine development. There are souls which naturally revolt from their surroundings and seem to belong to another age and clime. Let them be free to follow their bent; but the majority languish, become empty, become artificial, if artificially moulded into an alien form. It is God's arrangement that they should belong to a particular nation, age, society, that they should be children of the past, possessors of the present, creators of the future. The past is our foundation, the present our material, the future our aim and summit. Each must have its due and natural place in a National System of Education.

CHAPTER II
THE POWERS OF THE MIND

The instrument of the Educationist is the mind or *antahkarana*, which consists of four layers. The reservoir of past mental impressions, the *chitta* or storehouse of memory, which must be distinguished from the specific act of memory, is the foundation on which all the other layers stand. All experience lies within us as passive or potential memory ; active memory selects and takes what it requires from that storehouse. But the active memory is like a man searching among a great mass of locked-up material ; sometime he cannot find what he wants ; often in his rapid search he stumbles across many things for which he has no immediate need ; often too he blunders and thinks he has found the real thing when it is something else irrelevant if not valueless, on which he has laid his hand. The passive memory or *chitta* needs no training, it is automatic and naturally sufficient to its task ; there is not the slightest object of knowledge coming within its field which is not secured, placed and faultlessly preserved in that admirable receptacle. It is the active memory, a higher but less perfectly developed function, which is in need of improvement.

The second layer is the mind proper or *manas*, the sixth sense of our Indian Psychology, in which all the others are gathered up. The function of the mind is to receive the images of things translated into sight, sound, smell, taste and touch, the five senses and translate these again into thought-sensations. It receives also images of its own direct grasping and forms them into mental impressions. These sensations and impressions are the material of thought, not thought itself ; but it is exceedingly important that thought should work on sufficient and perfect material. It is therefore the first business of the Educationist, to develop in the child the right use of the six senses ; to see that they are not stunted or injured by disease, but trained by the child himself under the teacher's direction to that perfect accuracy and keen subtle sensitiveness of which they are capable. In addition, whatever assistance can be gained by the organs of action should be thoroughly employed. The hand, for instance, should be trained to reproduce what the eye sees, and the mind senses. The speech should be trained the perfect expression of the knowledge which the whole *antahkarna* possesses.

The third layer is the intellect or *buddhi*, which is the real instrument of thought and that which orders and disposes of the knowledge acquired by the other parts of the machine. For the purpose of the Educationist this is infinitely the most important of the three I have named. The intellect is an organ composed of several groups of functions, divisible into two important classes, the functions and faculties of the right hand, the functions and the faculties of the left hand. The faculties of the right hand are comprehensive, creative and synthetic; the faculties of the left hand critical and analytic. To the right hand belongs judgment, imagination, memory, observation; to the left hand comparison and reasoning.   The critical faculties distinguish, compare, classify, generalise, deduce, infer, conclude; they are the component parts of the logical reason. The right hand faculties comprehend, command, judge in their own right, grasp; hold and manipulate. The right hand mind is the master of the knowledge, the left hand its servant. The left hand touches only the body of knowledge, the right hand penetrates its soul. The left hand limits itself to assertained truth, the right hand grasps that which is still elusive or unascertained. Both are essential to the completeness of the human reason. These important functions of the machine have all to be raised to their highest and finest working-power, if the Education of the child is not to be imperfect and one-sided.

There is a fourth layer of faculty which, not as yet entirely developed in man, is attaining gradually a wider development and more perfect evolution. The powers peculiar to this highest stratum of knowledge are chiefly known to us from the phenomena of genius—sovereign discernment, intuitive perception of truth, plenary inspiration of speech, direct vision of knowledge to an extent often amounting to revelation, making a man a prophet of truth. The powers are rare in their higher development, though many possess them imperfectly or by flashes. They are still greatly distrusted by the critical reason of mankind because of the admixture of error, caprice and a biassed imagination which obstructs and distorts their perfect workings. Yet it is clear that humanity could not have advanced to its present stage if it had not been for the help of these faculties, and it is a question with which Educationists have not yet grappled, what is to be done with this mighty and baffling element, the element of genius in the pupil. The mere instructor does his best to discourage and stifle genius, the more liberal teacher welcoms it. Faculties so important to humanity cannot be left out of our consideration. It is foolish to neglect them. Their imperfect development must be perfected, the admixture of error, caprice and biassed fancifulness must be carefully and wisely removed. But the teacher cannot do it ; he would eradicate the good corn as well as the tares if he interfered. Here, as in all educational operations, he can only put the growing soul into the way of its own perfection.

CHAPTER III
THE MORAL NATURE

In the economy of man the mental nature rests upon the moral, and the education of the intellect divorced from the perfection of the moral and emotional nature is injurious to human progress. Yet, while it is easy to arrange some kind of curriculum or syllabus which will do well enough for the training of the mind, it has not yet been found possible to provide under modern conditions a suitable moral training for the School and College. The attempt to make boys moral and religious by the teaching of moral and religious text-books is a vanity and a delusion, precisely because the heart is not the mind and to instruct the mind does not necessarily improve the heart. It would be an error to say that it has no effect. It throws certain seeds of thought into the *antahkarana* and, if these thoughts become habitual, they influence the conduct. But the danger of moral text-books is that they make the thinking of high things mechanical and artificial, and whatever is mechanical and artificial, is inoperative for good.

There are three things which are of the utmost importance in dealing with a man's moral nature, the emotions, the *samskaras* or formed habits and associations, and the *swabhava* or nature. The only way for him to train himself morally is to habituate himself to the right emotions, the noblest associations, the best mental, emotional and physical habits and the following out in right action of the fundamental impulses of his essential nature. You can impose a certain discipline on children, dress them into a certain mould, lash them into a desired path, but unless you can get their hearts and natures on your side, the conformity to this becomes a hypocritical and heartless, often a cowardly compliance. This is what is done in Europe, and it leads to that remarkable phenomenon known as the sowing of wild oats as soon as the yoke of discipline at School and at home is removed, and to the social hypocrisy which is so large a feature of European life. Only what the man admires and accepts, becomes part of himself; the rest is a mask. He conforms to the discipline of society as he conformed to the moral routine of home and school, but considers himself at liberty to guide his real life, inner and private, according to his own likings and passions. On the other hand, to neglect moral and religious Education altogether is to corrupt the race. The notorious moral corruption in our young men previous to the saving touch of the Swadeshi Movement, was the direct result of the purely mental instruction given to them under the English System of Education. The adoption of the English System under an Indian disguise in Institutions like the Central Hindu College is likely to lead to the European result. That it is better than nothing, is all that can be said for it.

As in the education of the mind, so in the education of the heart, the best way is to put the child into the right road to his own perfection and encourage him to follow it, watching, suggesting, helping, but not interfering.

The one excellent element in the
English Boarding School is that the
master at his best stands there as a
moral guide and example, leaving the
boys largely to influence and help
each other in following the path
silently shown to them. But the
method practised is crude and marred
by the excess of outer discipline, for
which the pupils have no respect
except that of fear, and the exiguity
of the inner assistance. The little
good that is done is outweighed by
much evil. The old Indian System of
the *Guru* commanding by his knowledge and sanctity, the implicit
obedience, perfect admiration, reve-
rent emulation of the student, was a
far superior method of moral discipline. It is impossible to restore that
ancient system ; but it is not impossible to substitute the wise friend,

guide and helper for the hired Instructor or the benevolent Policeman which is all that the European System usually makes of the pedagogue.

The first rule of Moral Training is to suggest and invite, not command or impose. The best method of suggestion is by personal example, daily converse and the books read from day to day. These books should contain, for the younger student, the lofty examples of the past given, not as moral lessons, but as things of supreme human interest, and, for the elder student, the great thoughts of great souls, the passages of literature which set fire to the highest emotions and prompt the highest ideals and aspirations, the records of history and biography which exemplify the living of those great thoughts, noble emotions and aspiring ideals. This is a kind of good company, *saisanga*, which can seldom fail to have effect so long as sententious sermonising is avoided, and becomes of the highest effect if the personal life of the teacher is itself moulded by the great things he places before his pupils. It cannot, however, have full force unless the young life is given an opportunity, within its limited sphere, of embodying in action the moral impulses which rise within it. The thirst of knowledge, the self-devotion, the purity, the renunciation of the Brahmin, the courage, ardour, honour, nobility, chivalry, patriotism of the Kshatriya,—the beneficence, skill, industry, generous enterprise and large openhandedness of the Vaisya, —the self-effacement and loving service of the Sudra,—these are the qualities of the Aryan. They constitute the moral temper we desire in our young men, in the whole Nation. But how can we get them if we do not give opportunities to the young to train themselves in the Aryan tradition, to form by the practice and familiarity of childhood and boyhood the stuff of which their adult lives must be made?

Every boy should, therefore, be given practical opportunity as well as intellectual encouragement to develop all that is best in the nature. If he has bad qualities, bad habits, bad *samskaras* whether of mind or body, he should not be treated harshly as a delinquent, but encouraged to get rid of them by the Rajayogic Method of *Sanyama*, rejection and substitution. He should be encouraged to think of them, not as sins or offences, but as symptoms of a curable disease alterable by a steady and sustained effort of the will, falsehood being rejected whenever it rises into the mind and replaced by truth, fear by courage, selfishness by sacrifice and renunciation, malice by love. Great care will have to be taken that unformed virtues are not rejected as faults. The wildness and recklessness of many young natures are only the overflowings of an excessive strength, greatness and nobility. They should be purified, not discouraged.

I have spoken of morality; it is necessary to speak a word of religious teaching. There is a strange idea prevalent that by merely teaching the dogmas of religion children can be made pious and moral. This is an European error, and its practice leads, either to mechanical acceptance of a creed having no effect on the inner and little on the outer life, or it creates the fanatic, the pietist, the ritualist or the unctuous hypocrite. Religion has to be lived, not learned as a creed. The singular compromise made in the so-called National Education of Bengal making the teaching of religious beliefs compulsory, but forbidding the practice of *anushtana* or religious exercise, is a sample of the ignorant confusion which distracts men's mind on this subject. The prohibition is a sop to secularism declared or concealed. No religious teaching is of any value unless it is lived, and the use of various kinds of *sadhana*, spiritual self-training and exercise, is the only effective preparation for religious living. The ritual of prayer homage, ceremony is craved for by many minds as an essential preparation and, if not made an end in itself, is a great help to spiritual progress ; if it is withheld, some other form of meditation, devotion or religious duty must be put in its place. Otherwise, Religious Teaching is of little use and would almost be better ungiven.

But whether distinct teaching in any form of religion is imparted or not, the essence of religion, to live for God, for humanity, for country, for others and for oneself in these, must be made the ideal in every School which calls itself National. It is this spirit of Hinduism pervading our Schools which —far more than the teaching of Indian Subjects, the use of Indian methods or formal instruction in Hindu Beliefs and Hindu Scriptures—should be the essence of Nationalism in our Schools distinguishing them from all others.

CHAPTER IV
SIMULTANEOUS AND SUCCESSIVE TEACHING

A very remarkable feature of modern training which has been subjected in India to a reduction *ad absurdum* is the practice of teaching by snippets. A subject is taught a little at a time, in conjunction with a host of others, with the result that what might be well learnt in a single year is badly learned in seven and the boy goes out ill-equipped, served with imperfect parcels of knowledge, master of none of the great departments of human knowledge. The system of Education adopted by the National Council, an amphibious and twy-natured creation, attempts to heighten this practice of teaching by snippets at the bottom and the middle and suddenly change it to a grandiose specialism at the top.   This is to base the Triangle on its apex and hope that it will stand.

The old system was to teach one or two subjects well and thoroughly and then proceed to others, and certainly it was a more rational system than the modern. If it did not impart so much varied information, it built up a deeper, nobler and more real culture. Much of the shallowness, discursive lightness and fickle mutability of the average modern mind is due to the vicious principle of teaching by snippets.   The one defect that can be alleged against the old system was that the subject earliest learned might fade from the mind of the student while he was mastering his later studies. But the excellent training given to the memory by the ancients obviated the incidence of this defect. In the future

Education we need not bind ourselves either by the ancient or the modern system, but select only the most perfect and rapid means of mastering knowledge.

In defence of modern system it is alleged that the attention of children is easily tired and cannot be subjected to the strain of long application to a single subject. The frequent changes of subject gives rest to the mind. The question naturally arises: are the children of modern times then so different from the ancients, and, if so, have we not made them so by discouraging prolonged concentration ? A very young child cannot, indeed apply himself; but a very young child is unfit for School teaching of any kind. A child of seven or eight, and that is the earliest permissible age for the commencement of any regular kind of study, is capable of a good deal of concentration if he is interested. Interest is after all, the basis of concentration. We make his lessons supremely uninteresting and repellent to the child, a harsh compulsion the basis of teaching and then complain of his restless inattention ! The substitution of a natural self-Education by the child for the present unnatural system will remove this objection of inability. A child, like a man, if he is interested, much prefers to get to the end of his subject rather than leave it unfinished. To lead him on step by step, interesting and absorbing him in each as it comes, until he has mastered his subject is the true art of teaching.

The first attention of the teacher must be given to the medium and the instruments, and, until these are perfected, to multiply subjects of regular instruction is to waste time and energy. When the mental instruments are sufficiently developed to acquire a language easily and swiftly, that is the time to introduce him to many languages, not when he can only partially understand what he is taught and masters it laboriously and imperfectly. Moreover, one who has mastered his own language, has one very necessary facility for mastering another. With the linguistic faculty unsatisfactorily developed in one's own tongue, to master others is impossible. To study Science with the faculties of observation, judgment, reasoning, and comparison only slightly developed, is to undertake a useless and thankless labour. So it is with all other subjects.

The mother-tongue is the proper medium of Education and therefore the first energies of the child should be directed to the thorough mastering of the medium. Almost every child has an imagination, an instinct for words, a dramatic faculty, a wealth of idea and fancy. These should be interested in the literature and history of the Nation.   Instead of stupid and dry spelling and reading books, looked on as a dreary and ungrateful task, he should be introduced by rapidly progressive stages to the most interesting parts of his own literature and the life around him and behind him, and they should be put before him, in such a way as to attract and appeal to the qualities of which I have spoken. All other study at this period should be devoted to the perfection of the mental functions and the moral character.   A foundation should be laid at this time for the study of history, science, philosophy, art, but not in an obtrusive and formal manner. Every child is a lover of interesting narrative, a hero-worshipper and a patriot. Appeal to these qualities in him and through him, let him master without knowing it the living and human parts of his Nation's history. Every child is an inquirer, an investigator, analyser, a merciless anatomist. Appeal to those qualities in him and let him acquire without knowing it the right temper and the necessary fundamental knowledge of the Scientist. Every child has an insatiable intellectual curiosity and turn for metaphysical enquiry. Use it to draw him on slowly to an understanding of the world and himself. Every child has the gift of imitation and a touch of imaginative power. Use it to give him the ground work of the faculty of the artist.

It is by allowing Nature to work

that we get the benefit of the gifts she has bestowed on us. Humanity in its education of children has chosen to thwart and hamper the rapidity of its onward march. Happily, saner ideas are now beginning to prevail. But the way has not yet been found. The past hangs about our necks with all its prejudices and errors and will not leave us ; it enters into our most radical attempts to return to the guidance of the all-wise Mother. We must have the courage to take up clearer knowledge and apply it fearlessly in the interests of posterity. Teaching by snippets must be relegated to the lumber-room of dead sorrows. The first work is to interest the child in life, work and knowledge, to develop his instruments of knowledge with the utmost thoroughness, to give him mastery of the medium he must use.

Afterwards, the rapidity with which he will learn, will be found that, where now he learns a few things badly, then he will learn many things thoroughly well.

CHAPTER V
THE TRAINING OF THE MIND

There are six senses which minister to knowledge, sight, hearing, smell, touch and taste, mind, and all of these except the last, look outward and gather the material of thought from outside through the physical nerves and their end-organs, eye, ear, nose, skin, palate. The perfection of the senses as ministers to thought must be one of the first cares of the teachers. The two things that are needed of the senses are accuracy and sensitiveness. We must first understand what are the obstacles to the accuracy and sensitiveness of the senses, in order that we may take the best steps to remove them. The cause of imperfection must be understood by those who desire to bring about perfection.

The senses depend for their accuracy and sensitiveness on the unobstructed activity of the nerves which are the channels of their information and the passive acceptance of the mind which is the recipient.   In themselves the organs do their work perfectly.   The eye gives the right form, the ear the correct sound, the palate the right taste, the skin the right touch, the nose the right smell. This can easily be understood if we study the action of the eye as a crucial example.   A correct image is reproduced automatically on the retina, if there is any error in appreciating it, it is not the fault of the organ, but of something else.

The fault may be with the nerve currents. The nerves are nothing but channels, they have no power in themselves to alter the information given by the organs. But a channel may be obstructed and the obstruction may interfere either with the fullness or the accuracy of the information, not as it reaches the organ where it is necessarily and automatically perfect, but as it reaches the mind. The only exception is in case of a physical defect in the organ as an instrument. That is not a matter for the educationist, but for the physician.

If the obstruction is such as to stop the information reaching the mind at all, the result is an insufficient sensitiveness of the senses. The defects of sight, hearing, smell, touch, taste, anœthesia in its various degrees, are curable when not the effect of physical injury or defect in the organ itself. The obstructions can be removed and the sensitiveness remedied by the purification of the nerve system. The remedy is a simple one which is now becoming more and more popular in Europe for different reasons and objects, the regulation of the breathing. This process inevitably restores the perfect and unobstructed activity of the channels and, if well and thoroughly done, leads to a high activity of the senses. The process is called in Yogic discipline, *nadi-suddhi*, or nerve-purification.

The obstruction in the channel may be such as not absolutely to stop in however small a degree, but to distort the information. A familiar instance of this is the effect of fear or alarm on the sense action. The startled horse takes the sack on the road for a dangerous living thing, the startled man takes a rope for a snake, a waving curtain for a ghostly form. All distortions due to actions in the nervous system can be traced to some kind of emotional disturbance acting in the nerve channels. The only remedy for them is the habit of calm, the habitual steadiness of the nerves. This also can be brought about by *nadi-suddhi* or nerve-purficiation, which quiets the system, gives a deliberate calmness to all the internal processes and prepares the purification of the mind.

If the nerve channels are quiet and clear, the only possible disturbance of the information is from or through the mind. Now the *manas* or sixth sense is in itself a channel like the nerves, a channel for communication: with the *buddhi* or brainforce disturbance may happen either from above or from below. The information outside is first photographed on the end organ, then reproduced at the other end of the nerve system in the *chitta* or passive memory. All the images of sight, sound, smell, touch and taste are deposited there and the *manas* reports them to the *buddhi*. The *manas* is both a sense organ and a channel. As a sense organ it is as automatically perfect as the others, as a channel it is subject to disturbance resulting either in obstruction or distortion.

As a sense organ the mind receives direct thought impressions from outside and from within. These impressions are in themselves perfectly correct, but in their report to the intellect at all or may reach it so distorted as to make a false or partially false impression. The disturbance may effect the impression which attains the information of eye, ear, nose, skin or palate, but it is very slightly powerful here, in its effect on the direct impressions of the mind, it is extremely powerful and the chief source of error. The mind takes direct impressions primarily of thought, but also of form, sound, indeed of all the things for which it usually prefers to depend on the sense organs. The full development of this sensitiveness of the mind is called in our Yogic discipline *Sushmadrishti* or subtle reception of images. Telepathy, clairvoyance, claraudience, presentment, thought-reading, character-reading and many other modern discoveries are very ancient powers of the mind which have been left undeveloped, and they all belong to the *manas*. The development of the sixth sense has never formed part of human training. In a future age it will undoubtedly take a place in the necessary preliminary training of the human instrument. Meanwhile there is no reason why the mind should not be trained to give a correct report to the intellect so that our thought may start with absolutely correct if not with full impressions.

The first obstacle, the nervous emotional, we may suppose to be removed by the purification of the nervous system. The second obstacle is that of the emotions themselves warping the impressions as it comes. Love may do this, hatred may do this, any emotion or desire according to its power and intensity may distort the impression as it travels. This difficulty can only be removed by the discipline of the emotions, the purifying of the moral train-ing and its consideration may be postponed for the moment. The next difficulty is the interference of previous associations formed or in-grained in the *chitta* or passive memory. We have a habitual way of looking at things and the conservative inertia in our nature disposes us to give every new experience the shape and semblance of those to which we are accustomed. It is only more developed minds which can receive first impressions without an unconscious bias against the novelty of novel experience. For instance, if we get a true impression of what is happening and we habitually act on such impressions true or false if it differs from what we are accustomed to expect, the old association meets it in the *chitta* and sends a changed report to the intellect in which either the new impression is overlaid and concealed by the old or mingled with it. To go farther into this subject would be to involve ourselves too deeply into the details of psychology. This typical instance will suffice. To get rid of this obstacle is impossible without *chittasuddhi* or purification of the mental moral habits formed in the *chitta*. This is a preliminary process of Yoga and was effected in our ancient system by various means, but would be considered out of place in a modern system of education.

It is clear, therefore, that unless we revert to our old system in some of its principles, we must be content to allow this source of disturbance to remain. A really national system of education would not allow itself to be controlled by European ideas in this all important matter. And there is a process so simple and momentous that it can easily be made a part of our system.

It consists in bringing about passivity of the restless flood of thought sensations rising of its own momentum from the passive memory independent of our will and control. This passivity liberatest he intellect from the siege of old associations and false impressions. It gives it power to select only what is wanted from the storehouse of the passive memory, automatically brings about the habit of getting right impressions and enables the intellect to dictate so the *chitta* what *samskara* or associations shall be formed or rejected. This is the real office of the intellect to discriminate, choose, select, arrange. But so long as there is not *chitta-suddhi*, instead of doing this office perfectly, it itself remains imperfect and corrupt and adds to the confusion in the mind channel by false judgment, false imagination, false memory, false observation, false comparison, contrast and analogy, false education, induction and inference. The purification of the *chitta* is essential for the liberation, purification and perfect action of the intellect.

CHAPTER VI
SENSE-IMPROVEMENT BY PRACTICE

Another cause of the inefficiency of the senses as gatherers of Knowledge, is insufficient use. We do not observe sufficiently or with sufficient attention and closeness and a sight, sound, smell, even touch or taste knocks in vain at the door for admission. This *tamasic* inertia of the receiving instruments is no doubt due to the inattention of the *buddhi* and therefore its consideration may seem to come properly under the training of the functions of the intellect, but it is more convenient, though less psychologically correct, to notice it here. The student ought to be accustomed to catch the sights, sounds etc, around him, distinguish them, mark their nature, properties and sources and fix them in the *chitta* so that they may be always ready to respond when called for by the memory.

It is a fact which has been proved by minute experiments that the faculty of observation is very imperfectly developed in men, merely from want of care in the use of the sense and the memory. Give twelve men the task of recording from memory something they all saw two hours ago and the accounts will all vary from each other and from the actual occurence. To get rid of this imperfection will go a long way towards the removal of error. It can be done by training the senses to do their work perfectly which they will do readily enough if they know the *buddhi* requires it of them, and giving sufficient attention to put the facts in their right place and order in memory.

Attention is a factor in knowledge, the importance of which has been always recognised. Attention is the first condition of right memory and of accuracy. To attend to what he is doing, is the first element of discipline required of the student, and, as I have suggested, this can easily be secured if the object of attention is made interesting. This attention to a single thing is called concentration. One truth is however, sometimes overlooked ; that concentration on several things at a time is often indispensable. When people talk of concentration, they imply centring the mind on one thing at a time ; but it is quite possible to develop the power of double concentration, triple concentration, multiple concentration. When a given incident is happening, it may be made up of several simultaneous happenings or a set of simultaneous circumstances, a sight, a sound, a touch or several sights, sounds, touches occuring at the same moment or in the same short space of time. The tendency of the kind is to fasten on one and mark others vaguely, many not at all or, if compelled to attend to all, to be distracted and mark none perfectly. Yet this can be remedied and the attention equally distributed over a set of circumstances in such a way as to observe and remember each perfectly. It is merely a matter of *abhyasa* or steady natural practice.

It is also very desirable that the hand should be capable of coming to the help of the eye in dealing with the multitudinous objects of its activity so as to ensure accuracy. This is of a use so obvious and imperatively needed, that i t n e e d not be dwelt on at length. The practice of imitation by the hand of the thing seen is of use both of detecting the lapses and inaccuracies of the mind in noticing the objects of sense and in registering accurately what has been seen. Imitation by the hand ensures accuracy of observation. This is one of the first uses of drawing and it is sufficient in itself to make the teaching of this subject a necessary part of the training of the organs.

CHAPTER VII
THE TRAINING OF THE MENTAL FACULTIES

The first qualities of the mind that have to be developed are those which can be grouped under observation. We notice some things, ignore others. Even of what we notice, we observe very little. A general perception of an object is what we all usually carry away from a cursory half-attentive glance. A closer attention fixes its place, from nature as distinct from its surroundings. Full concentration of the faculty of observation gives us all the knowledge that the three chief senses can gather about the object, or if we touch or taste, we may gather all that the five senses can tell of its nature and properties. Those who make use of the six senses, the Poet, the Painter, the Yogin, can also gather much that is hidden from the ordinary observer. The Scientist by investigation ascertains other facts open to a minuter observation. These are the components of the faculty of observation, and it is obvious that its basis is attention, which may be only close, or close and minute. We may gather much even from a passing glance at an object, if we have the habit of concentrating the attention and the habit of *Satwic* receptivity. The first the teacher has to do is to accustom the pupil to concentrate attention.

We may take the instance of a flower. Instead of looking casually at it and getting a casual impression of scent, form and colour, he should be encouraged to know the flower—to fix in his mind the exact shade, the peculiar glow, the precise intensity of the scent, the beauty of curve and design in the form.   His touch should assure itself of the texture and its peculiarities.   Next, the flower should be taken to pieces and its structure examined with the same carefulness of observation.   All these should be done not as a task, but as an object of interest by skilfully arranged questions suited to the learner which will draw him on to observe and investigate one thing after the other until he has almost unconsciously mastered the whole.

Memory and judgment are the next qualities that will be called upon; and they should be encouraged in the same unconscious way.   The student should not be made to repeat the same lesson over again in order to remember it.   That is a mechanical burdensome and unintelligent way of training the memory. A similar but different flower should be put in the hands and he should be encouraged to note it with the same care, but with the avowed object of noting the similarities and differences. By this practice daily repeated the memory will naturally be trained. Not only so, but the mental centres of comparison and contrast will be developed. The learner will begin to observe as a habit the similarities of things and their differences. The teacher should take every care to encourage the perfect growth of this faculty and habit. At the same time, the laws of species and genus will begin to dawn on the mind and by a skilful follow-ing and leading of the young develop-ing mind, the scientific habit, the scientific attitude and the fundamental facts of scientific knowledge may in a very short time be made part of its permanent equipment.   The observation and comparison of flowers, leaves, plants, trees will lay the foundations of botanical knowledge without loading the mind with names and that dry, set acquisition of informations which is the beginning of cramming and detested by the healthy human mind when it is fresh from nature and unspoiled by natural habits. In the same way by the observation of the stars, astronomy, by the observation of earth, stones, etc., geology by the observation of insects and animals, etymology and zoology may be founded. A little later chemistry may be started by interesting observation of experiments without any formal teaching or heaping on the mind of formulas and book knowledge. There is no scientific object the perfect and natural mastery of which cannot be prepared in early childhood by this training of the faculties to observe, compare, remember and judge various classes of objects. It can be done easily and attended with a supreme and absorbing interest in the mind of the student. Once the taste is created, the boy can be trusted to follow it up with all the enthusiasm of youth in his leisure hours. This will prevent the necessity at a later age of teaching him everything in class.

The judgment will naturally be trained along with the other faculties. At every step the boy will have to decide what is the right idea, measurement, appreciation of colour, sound, scent, etc., and what is wrong. Often the judgments and distinctions made will have to be exceedingly subtle, and delicate. At first many errors will be made, but the learner should be taught to trust his judgment without being attached to its results. It will be found that the judgment will soon begin to respond to the calls made on it, clear itself of all errors and begin to judge correctly and minutely. The best way is to accustom the boy to compare his judgments with those of others. When he is wrong, it should at first be pointed out to him how far he was right and why he went wrong; afterwards he should be encouraged to note these things for itself. Every time he is right, his attention should be prominently and encouragingly called to it so that he may get confidence.

While engaged in comparing and contrasting, another centre is certain to develop, the centre of analogy.

The learner will inevitably draw ana-
logies and argue from like to like. He
should be encouraged to use his faculty
while noticing its limitations and
errors. In this way he will be trained
to form the habit of correct analogy
which is an indispensable and in the
acquisition of knowledge.

The one faculty we have omitted,
apart from the faculty of direct
reasoning, is Imagination. This is a
most important and indispensable
instrument. It may be divided into
three functions, the forming of mental
images, the power of creating thoughts
images and imitations or new combi-
nations of existing thoughts and
images, the appreciation of the soul in
things, beauty, charm, greatness, hidden suggestiveness, the emotion and
spiritual life that prevades the world.
This is in every way, as important as

the training of the faculties which observe and compare outward things. But I shall deal with it in a subsequent chapter.

The mental faculties should first be exercised on things, afterwards on words and ideas. Our dealings with language are much too perfunctory and the absence of a fine sense for words impoverishes the intellect and limits the fineness and truth of its operations. The mind should be accustomed first to notice the word thoroughly, its form, sound and sense ; then to compare the form with other similar forms in the points of similarity and difference, thus forming the foundation of the grammatical sense ; then to distinguish between the fine shades of sense of similar words and the formtaion and rhythm of different sentences ; thus the formation of the liberty and the syntactical faculties. All this should be done informally drawing on the curiosity and interest, avoiding set-teaching and memorising of rules. The true knowledge takes its base on things, *arthas*, and only when it has mastered the thing, proceeds to formalize its information.

CHAPTER VIII
THE TRAINING OF THE LOGICAL FACULTY

The training of the logical reason but necessarily follows the training of the faculties which collect the material on which the logical reason must work. Not only so but the mind must have some development of the faculty of dealing before it can deal successfully with ideas. The question is, once this preliminary work is done, what is the best way of teaching the boy to think correctly from premises. For the logical reason cannot proceed without premises. It either infers from facts to a conclusion to a fresh one, or from one fact to another. It either induces, deduces or simply infers. I see the Sun rise day after day, I conclude or induce that it rises to a law daily after a varying interval of darkness. I have already ascertained that wherever there is smoke, there is fire. I have induced that general rule from an observation of facts. I deduce that in a particular case of smoke, there is a fire behind. I infer that a man must have let it from the improbability of any other cause under the particular circumstances. I cannot deduce it because fire is not always created by human kindling ; it may be volcanic or caused by a stroke of lightening or the sparks from some kind of friction in the neighbourhood.

There are three elements necessary to correct reasoning: first, the correctness of the facts or conclusions I start from, secondly, the completeness as well as the accuracy of the data I start from, thirdly, the elimination of other possible or impossible conclu-

sions from the same facts.   The fallibility of the logical reason is due
partly to avoidable negligence and
looseness in securing these conditions,
partly to the difficulty of getting all
the facts correct, still more to the
difficulty of getting all the facts
complete, most of all, to the extreme
difficulty of eliminating all possible
conclusions except the one which
happens to be right.   No fact is supposed to be more perfectly established
than the universality of the Law of
Gravitation as an imperative rule, yet
a single new fact inconsistent with it
would upset this supposed universality. And such facts exist. Neverthe-
less by care and keenness the fallibility
may be reduced to its minimum.

The usual practice is to train the
logical reason by teaching the Science
of Logic.   This is an instance of the

prevalent error by which book knowledge of a thing is made the object of the study instead of the thing itself. The experience of reasoning and its errors should be given to the mind and it should be taught to observe how these work for itself; it should proceed from the example to the rule and from the accumulating harmony of rules to the formal science of the subject, not from the formal science to the rule, and from the rule to the example.

The first step is to make the young mind interest itself in drawing inferences from the facts, tracing cause and effect. It should then be led on to notice its successes and its failures and the reason of the success and of the failure; the incorrectness of the fact started from, the haste in drawing conclusions from insufficient facts, the carlessness in accepting a conclusion which is improbable, little supported by the data or open to doubt, the indolence or prejudice which does wish to consider other possible explanations or conclusions.   In this way the mind can be trained to reason as correctly as the fallibility of the human logic will allow, minimising the change of error.   The study of formal logic should be postponed to a later period when it can easily be mastered in a very brief period, since it will be only the systematising of the art perfectly well-known to the student.